Armadillo at Riverside Road

To Emily Rose — L.G.

To my sister, Annie, with love — K.B.

Illustration copyright © 1996 Katy Bratun.
Book copyright © 1996 Trudy Corporation, 353 Main Avenue, Norwalk, CT 06851,
and the Smithsonian Institution, Washington, DC 20560.

Soundprints is a division of Trudy Corporation, Norwalk, Connecticut.

Book Design: Shields & Partners, Westport, CT

First Edition 1996
10 9 8 7 6 5 4 3 2 1
Printed in Singapore

Acknowledgements:
   Our very special thanks to Dr. Charles Handley of the Department of Vertebrate Zoology at the
Smithsonian's National Museum of Natural History for his curatorial review.

Library of Congress Cataloging-in-Publication Data

Galvin, Laura Gates, 1963-

Armadillo at Riverside Road / written by Laura Gates Galvin ; illustrated by Katy Bratun.
          p.   cm.
Summary: Follows an armadillo on her nocturnal travels in search of food.
          ISBN 1-56899-328-5
1. Armadillos — Juvenile fiction. [1. Armadillos — Fiction.]
I. Bratun, Katy, ill. II. Title.
          PZ10.3.G153Ar 1996   96-7325
          [E] — dc20   CIP
                                                                              AC

Armadillo at Riverside Road

by Laura Gates Galvin

Illustrated by Katy Bratun

Soundprints
Where Children Discover...

A long summer day comes to an end as the sun slowly melts into the treetops. Silver maple leaves dance on their branches in a warm, gentle wind.

The sky is painted deep shades of red and orange — a sign that nighttime is near and soon there will be relief from the Texas heat.

Deep in a burrow behind the white house on Riverside Road, Armadillo wakes from a long day's sleep.

A breeze tickles Armadillo's small, leathery ears as she pokes her head out of her den. She pauses to feel for vibrations from footsteps nearby. All is quiet — it is safe to come out.

With strong legs, she pulls her body out of her hole. Then, she tiptoes through the tangle of blueberries and roses that hides her home. She is an odd sight — a stout little animal covered in a shield of armor.

Armadillo walks her funny walk, nervous and jerky, across the yard. With her nose to the ground, she plows through dirt and grass in hopes of finding a delicious bug or millipede. She gobbles a few crickets and moves on, teetering on four stubby legs with her long, armored tail trailing behind.

She snuffles and shuffles, snuffles and shuffles, looking for her meal. All of a sudden, Armadillo stops! Something under the soil smells delicious! With her sharp front claws, she digs a small hole and uncovers a feast of ants. Holding her breath so she won't breathe in dirt, she probes the ants' nest with her muzzle.

Armadillo reaches into the nest with her long, sticky tongue and brings a small mound of ant larvae to her mouth. Like a steam shovel she works her tongue back and forth until the entire nest is devoured.

The ants were good, but not enough to satisfy Armadillo's hunger. She pushes her nose back to the ground and continues hunting.

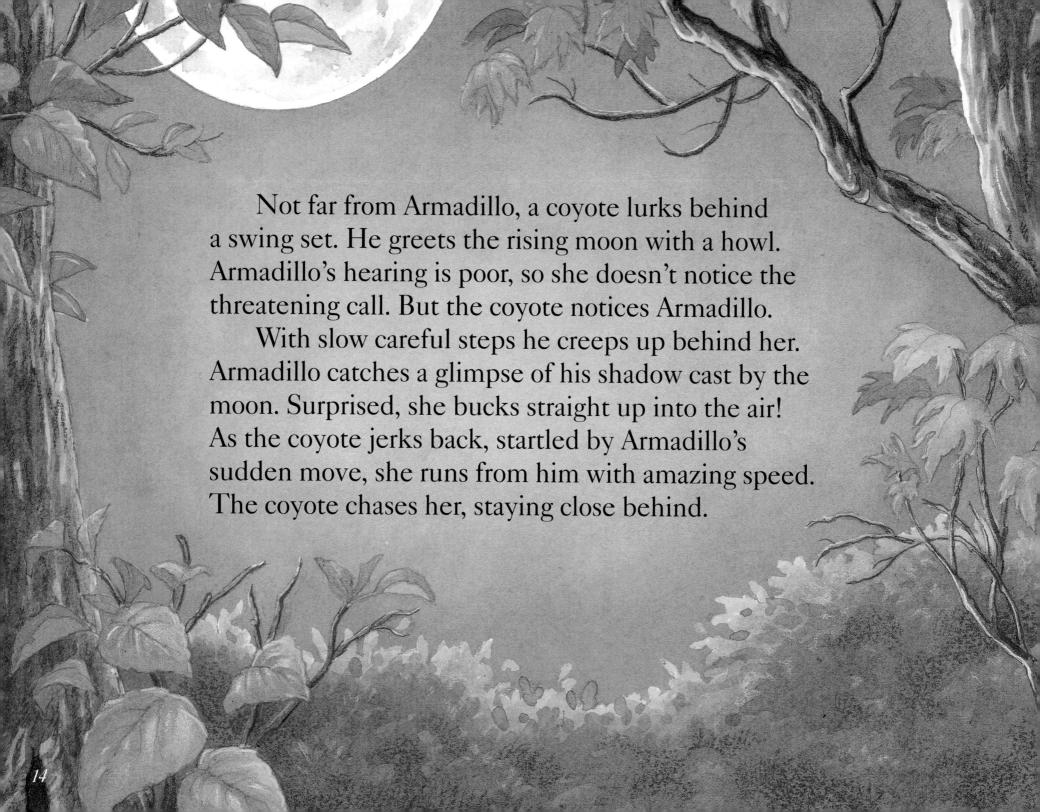

Not far from Armadillo, a coyote lurks behind a swing set. He greets the rising moon with a howl. Armadillo's hearing is poor, so she doesn't notice the threatening call. But the coyote notices Armadillo.

With slow careful steps he creeps up behind her. Armadillo catches a glimpse of his shadow cast by the moon. Surprised, she bucks straight up into the air! As the coyote jerks back, startled by Armadillo's sudden move, she runs from him with amazing speed. The coyote chases her, staying close behind.

Armadillo flees through a thorny thicket. Her armor protects her from the prickly plants. The coyote tries to follow, yelping as the sharp thorns stab his skin. Quickly, he backs out of the shrubs and runs around them, looking for Armadillo. She is nowhere to be found.

Armadillo runs to a nearby stream and hurries in.
She sinks to the bottom like a stone and walks underwater.
As she comes up on the far bank, the coyote spots her.
He dashes to the stream and leaps across. In a flash, he
catches up to her.

18

Just as the coyote opens his jaws to take a bite of Armadillo, she disappears into the ground. She has found safety in one of her many burrows.

Armadillo stays underground as the coyote paces back and forth above her. Waiting for the coyote to give up, she falls asleep.

Late in the night, Armadillo awakens. She is hungry again, and climbs out of the burrow to search for more food.

She discovers many insects roaming near the stream. Walking alongside the water, she eats every bug in her path.

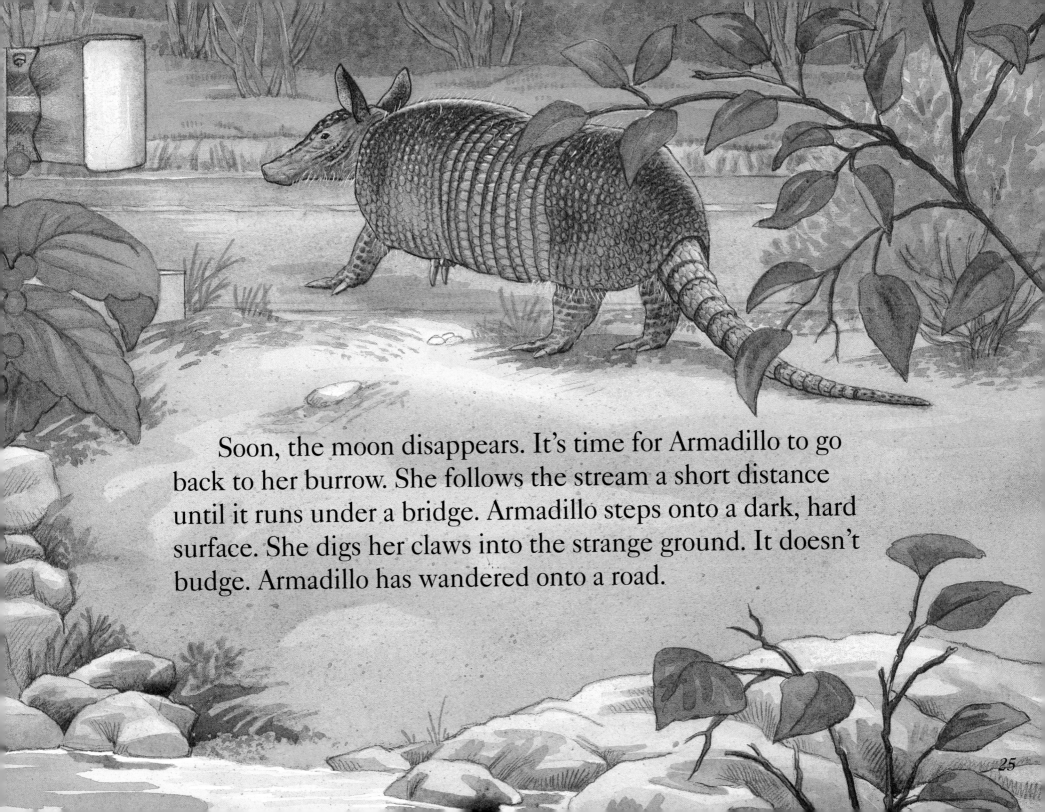

Soon, the moon disappears. It's time for Armadillo to go back to her burrow. She follows the stream a short distance until it runs under a bridge. Armadillo steps onto a dark, hard surface. She digs her claws into the strange ground. It doesn't budge. Armadillo has wandered onto a road.

Confused, Armadillo takes a few steps and tries digging again. Her claws only scratch the pavement.

Suddenly, the silence of early morning is broken by an approaching roar and two beams of bright light.

Whoosh! A blast of air hits Armadillo's face as a car speeds by. The force of the air knocks her over and off the road. She scrambles to her feet and finds herself near the stream again.

Armadillo walks to the water's edge. As she steps in, the gentle current carries her away. With deep breaths of air she inflates her body like a balloon and floats downstream. When the water becomes more shallow, she digs her claws into soft mud and pulls herself out onto the opposite bank.

As the sun begins to rise, Armadillo hurries through a thicket and across a familiar backyard.

The sky is streaked with pink and purple clouds.
A mockingbird greets the morning with a song. Deep
in her burrow behind the white house on Riverside
Road, Armadillo settles onto a soft bed of grass.

As the August sun becomes brighter and the air
becomes warmer, Armadillo grows tired. She closes
her eyes, ready for a long day's sleep.

About the Nine-banded Armadillo

Nine-banded armadillos, also called common long-nosed armadillos, are found from the southeastern United States into Mexico, Central America, and South America.

During hot weather, armadillos avoid heat and sun by sleeping in burrows during the day and hunting at night. With poor eyesight and hearing, they rely on their keen senses of smell to find food. Ants are one of their favorites and they can eat up to 40,000 in one meal. Armadillos are also important predators of beetles.

In early spring, mother armadillos give birth to quadruplets — four identical babies. The babies are born with soft, leathery skin which hardens within a few weeks into armor on the head, back, and tail. The armor protects them from the teeth and claws of predators, as well as thorny plants. Baby armadillos are weaned from their mothers and learn to hunt on their own two or three weeks after birth. They grow to approximately 2-1/2 feet long, including the length of their tails. Nine movable bands in the middle of their bodies allow them to bend and move easily.

Glossary

armor: a hard, protective body covering.

burrow: a hole in the ground dug by an animal for use as a home or shelter.

coyote: an animal, resembling a german shepherd dog, closely related to the wolf.

inflates: becomes swollen with air.

larvae: the young, wingless forms that hatch from eggs of insects.

millipede: a small animal, related to insects, that has a long, cylinder-shaped body and 50 to 100 pairs of legs.

mockingbird: a songbird known for its ability to mimic the calls of other birds.

muzzle: the jaws and nose of an animal.

thicket: a thick growth of trees or shrubs.

Points of Interest in this Book

pp. 4-5 evening primrose (white flower), dandelions.

pp. 8-9 field cricket, black-eyed susans, evening primrose, blue toadflax.

pp. 10-11 butterfly pea (pink flower at left), dandelion, common gray tree frog, fire ants.

pp. 12-13 zig-zag ruel (blue flower), katydid, creeping buttercup, ten-lined June beetle.

pp. 16-17 chickasaw plum.

pp. 18-19 arrowheads (broad leaves at top).

pp. 20-21 Texas sleepy aster (yellow flower).

pp. 22-23 elegant checkered beetle, alutacea bird, grasshopper, cattails, green frog.

pp. 24-25 penitent underwing moth.

✓ *pp. 30-31* white-footed mouse.